Hey Jack! Books

First American Edition 2013
Kane Miller, A Division of EDC Publishing

Text copyright © 2012 Sally Rippin
Illustration copyright © 2012 Stephanie Spartels
Logo and design copyright © 2012 Hardie Grant Egmont

First published in Australia in 2012 by Hardie Grant Egmont

For information contact:
Kane Miller, A Division of EDC Publishing
P.O. Box 470663
Tulsa, OK 74147-0663
www.kanemiller.com
www.edcpub.com
www.usbornebooksandmore.com

Library of Congress Control Number: 2012931657

Printed and bound in the United States of America
3 4 5 6 7 8 9 10
ISBN: 978-1-61067-126-2

Hey Jack!

The Worry Monsters

By Sally Rippin

Illustrated by Stephanie Spartels

Kane Miller
A DIVISION OF EDC PUBLISHING

Chapter One

This is Jack.

Today Jack is feeling

worried. His class

has a spelling test

next week.

Jack is good at math
and art, but terrible
at spelling. He can't
understand why *too*, *to*
and *two* are all spelled
differently. Spelling
makes no sense!

Jack has 24 words
to remember.

Outside it is **sunny**, and Jack's puppy wants to play. Jack pushes the list of words to the bottom of his bag. He will worry about the spelling test later.

Jack and Scraps play

outside in the backyard.

They laugh and

bark and roll

around on the grass.

Soon it is time

to go inside for dinner.

Jack's mom has cooked

his favorite – pasta!

She gives him an
extra-big serving.

"Did you get any
school handouts today?"
Jack's mom asks.

Suddenly Jack
remembers the list
of words at the
bottom of his bag.

His tummy squeezes
tight. He looks down
at his plate.

"Um… no," he says.

Jack doesn't want to think about the spelling test. It makes his tummy **hurt**. He tries to finish his dinner, but the pasta doesn't taste so good anymore.

7

That night, Jack lies

awake in the dark.

The worries in

his tummy are getting

bigger and bigger.

They feel like

big scary monsters

that are whispering

mean things to him.

Jack turns on the light.

He gets out of bed and

goes to his school bag.

The list of words is

still **scrunched**

up at the bottom.

But then Jack sees the

comic book he got

from the school library.

10

Jack snuggles back
into bed with the
comic book.

There is still a

whole week until

the test. He will worry

about it tomorrow.

Chapter Two

All that week Jack

is very busy. At school

he plays soccer with

his friend Billie.

After school he plays with Scraps.

On the weekend he and Billie build a huge pirate ship from chairs and broomsticks and bedsheets.

On Sunday night Jack packs his bag for school.

14

At the bottom of

the bag is a scrunched-

up piece of paper.

Oh no! The spelling test.

Jack has forgotten to

study the words.

And the test is tomorrow!

Jack feels his tummy

shrink with worry.

16

He pulls out the test

and looks at it.

There are so many

tricky words on there.

Jack knows he will get them all wrong. He stuffs it back into his bag and crawls into bed.

That night he imagines the worry monsters in his room again. This time they are even bigger and scarier than before.

18

The next morning Jack
feels sick in his tummy.
He doesn't want to
go to school.

He wants to tell his
mom about the test.
But he is worried that
she will be **cross**
with him.

Jack walks to school

with Billie and her mom.

He is very quiet.

"Is something wrong?"

Billie asks.

"No," says Jack,

shaking his head.

"Are you sure?" says Billie.

"I'm fine," says Jack

crossly. He wishes Billie

would stop asking.

In class, Jack's tummy ache starts to **hurt** even more.

"I don't feel well," Jack says to Billie.

Billie puts up her hand. "Ms. Walton," she says. "Jack doesn't feel well. Can I take him to the nurse?"

22

"Oh dear," Ms. Walton says.

"You do look a little

pale, Jack."

"Billie will take you to the nurse. I'll call your parents. You'll miss the spelling test, but you can do it tomorrow."

Jack lies in the nurse's office waiting to be picked up. Billie waits with him.

24

"Can I tell you
something?" Jack says.

"Sure," says Billie.
"What is it?"

"I didn't study the
spelling words," Jack says.
"I don't know what
to tell Mom and Dad."

"Just tell them
the truth," Billie says.

Jack lies back. There are
patterns on the ceiling
that remind him of
the worry monsters.
He closes his eyes
to make them go away.

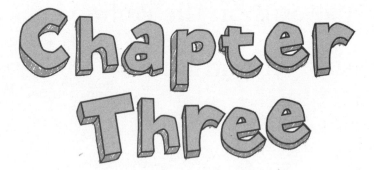

Chapter Three

At home, Jack's dad

tucks him into bed.

He puts a cold washcloth

on Jack's forehead.

"So," his dad says kindly.

"Do you want to tell me

what's wrong?"

Jack hangs his head.

"I had a spelling test today. I forgot to study the words."

"You forgot?" says his dad. He lifts his eyebrows and **smiles**.

Jack sighs. "I'm terrible at spelling, Dad," he says in a little voice. "I just can't do it!"

"That doesn't sound like
my Jack," his dad says.
He gives Jack a cuddle.
"Why don't we study the
words together?"

31

"You will have to go
back to school sometime,
and the spelling test
will still be there."

Jack climbs out of
bed. He pulls the
wrinkled paper
from his school bag
and hands it to his dad.

His dad reads the words.

"Hmmm. Some of these are

tricky," he says. "But I have

an idea. Come and help

me with some cooking."

33

Jack looks surprised.

"But I thought we were going to study my spelling words?" he says.

"We are!" says his dad.

Jack follows his dad
into the kitchen.

"Right," says his dad.
"First course is
alphabet soup.
Then words on
bread and cookies
shaped like letters.

35

We are going to
practice those words
then eat them up when
we get them right."

Jack laughs. This sounds
like **fun**!

All afternoon Jack and
his dad make words
out of cookies, pasta
and even cut-up fruit.

When they have

eaten all the food,

Jack and his dad

practice with a pencil

and paper. Soon Jack

knows all the words

by heart. He can't

wait to take the test

tomorrow!

That night Jack

lies in bed and waits

for the worry monsters

to come. When they do,

he is ready for them.

"Go away!" he says.

"I've studied

my words for the

spelling test."

39

The worry monsters

disappear.

Jack knows they

will come back again

someday. But he

also knows that

he doesn't need

to be **afraid**

of them anymore.

40

41

When Jack takes his spelling test the next day, Ms. Walton is very surprised.

"My goodness, Jack!" she says. "You have improved. Well done!"

"Wow!" Billie says when she sees his grade.

"How did you remember all those words?"

"I'll teach you a trick my dad taught me," Jack grins. "But I hope you like alphabet soup!"